The Littles
Go Exploring

The Littles
Go Exploring

by John Peterson

Interior Illustrations by
Roberta Carter Clark

SCHOLASTIC INC.

Copyright © 1978 by John Peterson
Illustrations copyright © 1978 by Scholastic Inc.

All rights reserved. Published by Scholastic Inc., *Publishers since 1920.* SCHOLASTIC and associated logos are trademarks and/or registered trademarks of Scholastic Inc.

The publisher does not have any control over and does not assume any responsibility for author or third-party websites or their content.

No part of this publication may be reproduced, stored in a retrieval system, or transmitted in any form or by any means, electronic, mechanical, photocopying, recording, or otherwise, without written permission of the publisher. For information regarding permission, write to Scholastic Inc., Attention: Permissions Department, 557 Broadway, New York, NY 10012.

This book is a work of fiction. Names, characters, places, and incidents are either the product of the author's imagination or are used fictitiously, and any resemblance to actual persons, living or dead, business establishments, events, or locales is entirely coincidental.

ISBN 978-1-338-30996-6

10 9 8 7 6 5 4 3   19 20 21 22 23

Printed in the U.S.A.   40
This edition first printing, 2019

Book design by Lizzy Yoder
Interior illustrations by Roberta Carter Clark

To Aunt Win

Tom and Lucy Little stood on the roof of the Biggs's house. They watched Cousin Dinky's glider climb high into the sky and disappear beyond the trees. A minute before, they had seen Cousin Dinky zoom down and drop a letter into the Biggs's chimney.

This was the way the Little family always got their mail. They had put a net across the chimney to keep the letters from falling into the fireplace below.

The children ran to pick up the letter — but the net was empty!

"Hey!" said Tom. "There *was* a letter, wasn't there?"

TOM   LUCY   MR. LITTLE   MRS. LITTLE

Lucy pointed. "Look, Tom," she said. "There's a hole in the net. The letter must have fallen through."

"Wait," said Tom. "Look down there — inside the chimney."

Lucy Little lay flat on her stomach on top of the chimney. She peered into the darkness below. "I see *something* white," she said. "Is that the letter? Where is it?"

"It must be stuck on one of the bricks," said Tom. "I'm going to climb down there and get it."

"Tom!" said Lucy. "Are you sure? You might fall into the fireplace and get hurt — or the Biggs might see you. What would happen to us then?"

To be seen by the Biggs would be the worst thing that could happen to Lucy and Tom and their whole family. That's

because the Littles were tiny people. (The biggest Little was just six inches tall.) The Littles lived secretly inside the walls of the house owned by George W. Bigg and his family.

There were eight Littles in all: Tom, who was ten years old; Lucy, who was eight; their parents, Mr. and Mrs. William T. Little; their baby sister; their grandmother; and their two uncles. There was plenty of room for everybody in their comfortable ten-room apartment inside the walls of the Biggs's house.

In most ways, the tiny Littles were like ordinary-sized people — except for one thing. They had tails. The Littles thought their tails were handsome. And they thought big people looked very strange *without* tails.

Maybe big people would think the Littles looked strange too — but no big person had ever seen a Little. The Littles wanted to keep it that way. And so did all the other tiny families who lived in houses in the Big Valley. They always stayed out of sight in their houses, and they hardly ever went out to visit each other. To keep in touch, they sent letters.

Cousin Dinky Little, a pilot, delivered everyone's mail. He loved to travel up and down the Big Valley in his glider. He and his wife, Della, flew everywhere together, delivering the mail and having adventures.

Tom and Lucy always looked forward to getting the mail. Now a letter had fallen down into the chimney!

"I've got to get that letter," Tom said, and he started to go down. Suddenly, he stopped.

"Hey, Lucy," he said. "I never noticed it before, but these bricks are almost like steps. It's easy to climb down. Kind of hot, though."

"Wait, Tom," said Lucy. "I'm going with you."

The tiny girl followed her brother into the chimney. It was dark and sooty.

Five feet down, the "steps" came to a stop. The letter lay on the last step. Tom picked it up and sat down on the step.

"Who's the letter from?" Lucy asked.

Tom held the letter close to his eyes. He could just make out the writing in the dim light.

"Oh — it's for you," said Tom. He handed his sister the letter. "From your best friend."

"Tina?" said Lucy. "Oh, good!"

Tom leaned back against the chimney. "Hey!" he yelled.

"What's wrong?" said Lucy.

"It moved!"

"What moved?"

Tom jumped to his feet. "This brick I leaned against — it moved!" The boy began to push the brick.

"Tom — be careful," Lucy warned. "The chimney might fall down if there's a loose brick."

"But, look — it moves," said Tom. "See?" He pushed the brick. A tiny crack of light came from behind the

brick. Tom pushed again. This time
Lucy helped him.

Light flooded into the dark chimney.

"This is crazy," said Tom, almost
whispering. He stuck his head through
the opening. "It's a *room!*"

"A room?" Lucy said. "Oh, Tom — a
secret room!"

The children walked into the tiny
room. The light was coming through a
little window which was set into the far
wall of the room.

Tom and Lucy looked about them. They saw a small table and a chair in the room — just like the ones the Littles had in their apartment. The table was covered with papers.

Lucy ran to the window and looked out. "There's the Biggs's yard," she said. "But where are we, Tom? Where is this room?"

"It must be *behind* the chimney in the attic," Tom said.

"Whose room is it?" said Lucy. "We've never seen it before."

Tom picked up some of the papers from the table. He blew off some dust. "It was used by a tiny person, that's for sure. But no one's been here for a long time," he said.

"Tom," said Lucy in her quietest voice, "let's keep it a secret. Let's not tell *anyone*. It can be our secret room."

Tom looked down at the yellow papers. He shook his head. "We can't

do that," he said. "We'll have to tell
Mother and Dad right away."

"Why?" asked Lucy. "What did you
find, Tom?"

"These papers belong to *Grandpa
Little*, that's why," answered Tom. "This
room — he must have come here and no
one knew."

"Grandpa Little?" said Lucy. "But he
. . . he disappeared a couple of years ago.
Everyone says he's probably dead."

Lucy sat down in the chair.

" . . . everyone *except* Granny Little,"
she went on. "She thinks he's alive
someplace, doesn't she? I think she
does. But she never talks about him.
Didn't she like Grandpa?"

"There never was a clue," said Tom.
"Not one teeny clue about what
happened to Grandpa when he disappeared."

Tom looked at Lucy. "Gee — maybe
there's something in all these old papers
that tells." He held up a bunch of the
papers. "Look — here's some kind of
diary, and some maps. We have to tell
Mother and Dad right away. But, Lucy
— we can't tell Granny."

"Why not?"

"She's funny about Grandpa. Dad will
have to decide what to do."

"But why shouldn't she know? It's her
husband!"

"You just said that Granny thinks Grandpa is still alive," said Tom. "I'll bet she doesn't, really. But she won't talk about him, ever."

"Well, does that mean . . .?"

"Dad says that if someone you loved just disappeared — that's worse than if he had died," Tom went on. "You would hope he was alive, but you'd think maybe he was dead. Just wondering about it would be awful."

"Do you mean that's why she won't talk about it?" asked Lucy. "She doesn't want to think about it?"

"Yeah, I suppose so," Tom answered. "I guess that's it."

"You know, it bothers me, too," said Lucy, "that Grandpa just . . . just disappeared."

"I don't understand it," said Uncle Pete. "What difference does it make if Grandpa had a secret room and a diary and a bunch of maps? He's dead — we all know that."

"Not so loud, Uncle Pete," said Mr. Little.

"We don't want Granny to know about what we found — not yet," Mrs. Little said.

The Littles were in the living room in their apartment inside the walls. Mrs. Little was changing Baby Betsy's diaper. Uncle Pete was limping back and forth in front of the fireplace. (He had been wounded in the Mouse Invasion of '35 and had walked with a limp ever since.)

Uncle Nick, who used to be a soldier in the Mouse Force Brigade, was looking over the papers Tom and Lucy had found. "Very interesting, very interesting," he said.

"*Interesting*, sure," Uncle Pete said. "All that stuff can go into the Little Family History Book."

"Makes sense, makes sense," said Uncle Nick, talking to himself.

"Well, why shouldn't it make sense?" Uncle Pete went on. "Grandpa was smart. Why, he was the first Little to understand electricity. And that's why we could help the Biggs with electrical problems from inside the walls without their knowing about it."

Mr. Little nodded. "Grandpa had a lot of good ideas," he said.

"Yet he was strange in a way," said Uncle Pete. "He liked to be alone a lot. Now we find out he even had a secret room. But that doesn't mean any of these papers we found can tell us anything about why he disappeared."

"Maybe he ran away," Lucy said.

"Lucy!" said Mrs. Little. "What an idea!"

"Look at these papers, Will," said Uncle Nick. "I think I've found some clues that might help us find out what happened to the old man."

"Clues, my foot!" said Uncle Pete. He stomped over to his favorite chair and sat down hard. "We looked *everywhere* after Grandpa disappeared. He's gone. That's all there is to it. Probably eaten by a dog or something. We'll never know."

"Ugh," said Lucy.

Mrs. Little put her arm around Lucy. "Please, Uncle Pete — don't say such things," she said.

Mr. Little read the papers. "Let's see," he said. "In this part of the diary he tells about a trip he made when he was a boy. He went down the brook by raft to the Dark Woods. He tells how much he enjoyed 'going exploring.' Then he says, '*I would like to find out more about this part of the Big Valley.* . . . *What lies beyond the Dark Woods? No tiny person has ever gone there.*'"

"Nonsense!" shouted Uncle Pete from across the room. "Cousin Dinky knows what's over there."

"No, he doesn't, Uncle Pete," said Tom. "Cousin Dinky's never flown over there. He told me so."

Mr. Little went on: "Here's a map of the place as Grandpa remembered it. He's put a big question mark on the part of the map beyond the Dark Woods."

"Now look at this," said Uncle Nick. He took a paper from Mr. Little and held it up for everyone to see.

Uncle Pete limped across the room and grabbed the paper from Uncle Nick's hand. He stared at it. "What is this anyhow?" he said. "Why, you can't even read the writing. It looks like gobble-de-gook to me."

"It's mirror-writing," Uncle Nick said. He held the drawing up to the mirror over the fireplace. "It says, *'Plan for submarine raft to make the exploring trip.'* "

"Wow!" Tom said. "A submarine raft! It's terrific! Look — it's made from a bottle . . . a glass bottle."

Uncle Pete spoke: "It doesn't prove a thing!" he said. "No one would make a trip like that by himself."

Mrs. Little nodded. "It could be just an idea he had," she said.

"Read the last paper, Will," said Uncle Nick.

"It's from Grandpa's diary again," Mr. Little said. "He says, *'I may have to make the trip alone. I'm the one who wants to explore the place. It wouldn't be fair to ask someone else to go. It will be dangerous. Some of the family might think I'm too old, but they are wrong. I'll never be too old to go exploring!'* "

"Okay . . . okay!" said Uncle Pete. "Don't read any more." He leaned against the mantelpiece. "Why didn't he tell us? We could have helped him."

"Now, Uncle Pete, you know we would have tried to talk him out of it," said Mr. Little.

"If only he had told us!" Uncle Pete said. He took out his handkerchief and wiped a tear from his eye. "I could have gone with him."

Late that afternoon, Cousin Dinky and his wife, Della, landed their glider on the Biggs's roof. They had finished delivering the mail.

Cousin Dinky liked to visit the Littles at dinner time. The food was always delicious. Meals at the Littles came from Mrs. Bigg's kitchen. She made such good meals that Mrs. Little never bothered learning how to cook. The Littles simply took what they wanted from the Biggs.

The Biggs didn't know that an electric socket at their kitchen counter was a secret door. The Littles just slipped through the door and grabbed whatever leftovers they wanted. It didn't take much food to feed the Littles and their guests. The Biggs never missed it.

After supper, Granny Little went off to bed. Mrs. Little fed and burped Baby Betsy. She put her to bed in the matchbox cradle.

Once again the talk turned to Grandpa Little. What could have happened to him when he went out into the Dark Woods alone?

"Dinky and I could fly over by the Dark Woods," said Della, "to see what we could see."

"It's been two years since Grandpa went away," said Mr. Little. "You may not find any clues."

"That submarine raft may be at the bottom of the brook," Uncle Pete said. "You'd never see that from up in the glider."

Uncle Nick stood up. "There's only one way to find out what really happened to Grandpa. I will explore the brook," he said. "I'll need two volunteers to go along."

"I'll go," said Tom.

"Tom!" said Mrs. Little. "You'll do no such thing."

"What's the use?" asked Uncle Pete. "He's dead, that's for sure."

"He *might* be alive, Uncle Pete," said Lucy. She took her uncle's hand.

"We should look anyway," said Tom.

"I think Granny Little needs to know what happened to her husband," said Della. "If there's the smallest chance we can find out, we should try."

Mrs. Little nodded.

"Granny doesn't say anything about it," Della went on, "but you can tell it upsets her not to know."

Suddenly Mrs. Little stood up. "That settles it!" she said. "Della is right."

Everyone looked surprised. They had never heard Mrs. Little talk this way.

"I have to speak for Granny," she went on. "She's not here to speak for herself. Now — *this* is what we should do."

Mrs. Little took a deep breath. "Somehow . . . somehow we're *all* going to go and look for . . . whatever it is we're looking for. Every one of us! Until we find out what happened to that dear old man. We're going to do it for Granny. Because she works so hard for every one of us . . . especially *me!*" Mrs. Little sat down. "There!" she said.

Mr. Little smiled. "Mrs. Little has spoken," he said.

Lucy kissed her mother "You were great, Mother," she said.

"Then it's decided," Uncle Nick said. "Instead of a small three-man expedition as I suggested, we'll put together the biggest and best tiny people's expedition ever."

Uncle Pete sat up. "Well, if you're all set on going, I'll go too," he said. "Someone will have to look after the weapons. There will be danger. We'll need to be strongly armed."

Uncle Nick held up some maps. "I'll map the way," he said. "We'll search every nook and cranny of the brook."

"Hooray!" shouted Lucy. "Let's go and wake up Granny and tell her the news. The Littles are going exploring!"

"There," Tom said. He pointed. "There's Henry Bigg's sailboat. He left it there a week ago."

Tom, Lucy, Mr. Little, and Uncle Pete were under a bush. They were near the pond behind the Biggs's house. There was a toy sailboat tied near the shore of the pond.

"It's a beauty!" said Uncle Pete.

"Tom — I'm glad you remembered this," said Mr. Little. "I think all of us could travel comfortably on that sailboat. And, there's plenty of room for any supplies we might need. We're going to borrow it for our exploring trip down the brook."

Mr. Little looked across the pond. "Right now we have to get the boat over that dam and into the brook," he said. "We'll keep it anchored in the brook until everything is ready for the trip."

"Let's get going!" said Uncle Pete. He started for the boat.

Uncle Pete, Mr. Little, and Lucy climbed into the toy sailboat. Tom untied the string that held the boat near shore and hopped on.

The boat moved slowly out into the pond. A light breeze came up and puffed out the sail.

Uncle Pete stood in the front of the boat. "Yo-ho-ho and a bottle of cola!" he sang.

Mr. Little steered the boat toward the dam. All at once they heard a strange sound. Lucy pointed to the sail. "Look," she said. "The sail is flopping around up there."

"I can fix that," said Tom. He ran to the mast and started climbing.

"Careful, Tom," called Mr. Little.

"I can tighten this string in a minute," said Tom from the top of the mast.

"*Daddy!*" whispered Lucy. "Look!" The tiny girl pointed.

"Oh, oh," said Mr. Little.

There were two boys and a girl on the shore of the pond. They had on bathing suits.

"It's Henry Bigg," said Mr. Little.

"And two of his cousins," added Lucy.

The three big children were pushing a rowboat out into the pond. They climbed into it.

Uncle Pete walked over to Mr. Little and Lucy. "We'd better get off this boat," he whispered, "and try another day."

"Right," Mr. Little said. "Let's go."

"Wait, Daddy," said Lucy. "What about Tom?"

"Tom!" called Mr. Little in a loud whisper. He didn't want the big children to hear.

Tom kept right on working.

Just then the tall girl dived from the rowboat into the water.

Tom heard the splash. He looked over and saw the girl swimming. Tom started down the mast.

The girl swam toward the sailboat. "I'll get the sailboat, Henry," she called. "We'll have some fun with it."

"Everybody off the boat!" Mr. Little said. He and Lucy and Uncle Pete dived into the water on the far side of the sailboat where the girl couldn't see them. They swam to some lily pads and hid.

Tom got to the bottom of the mast just as the girl got to the boat. It was too late for Tom to get off now. The girl would surely see him. What could he

do? Tom looked for a place to hide. He saw a hole — in the floor of the boat. Just in time he jumped in. He landed in a dark room in the belly of the boat.

Poor Tom Little! He stayed in the belly of that sailboat for an hour. Henry and his cousins sailed the boat back and forth over the pond. Once some water splashed into the room where Tom was hiding. Henry picked up the sailboat. He turned it over to empty out the water. He shook the boat. It was all Tom could do to hold on and not fall out.

"What if . . . " said one of Henry's cousins, "what if we were so small we could ride in the sailboat. Wouldn't that be great?"

"Oh, yeah," said Tom to himself. "Great." By this time he was very seasick.

Afterwards, when the big children left, Tom made his way to the edge of the pond. Mr. Little, Uncle Pete, and Lucy were waiting for him.

"Tom, you look *awful*," said Lucy.

"Why can't we *walk* on our exploring trip?" asked Tom.

The four Littles went back to the apartment in the walls of the house. Cousin Dinky, Della, and Uncle Nick were waiting for them. They had been traveling around in Cousin Dinky's glider.

"We found a boat," Cousin Dinky said.

"It's beautiful!" said Della.

"Large enough to take us all exploring," Uncle Nick joined in.

"Oh no," Tom said. "I think I'm going to be sick again."

For the next few weeks the Littles got
ready for the trip. There was much to
do.

The boat was in the brook just below
the pond. It was a toy boat stuck in some
weeds near the shore. Mr. Little, Uncle
Nick, Tom, and Cousin Dinky went
down to pull it out of the weeds.

"It's perfect," Mr. Little said.

The boat was made of plastic. It was
more than a foot and a half long. There
were two floors (or decks) — upper and
lower. On the upper deck was a chair
and a wheel for steering the boat. There
was a flagpole and a plastic flag.

Most of the room on the lower deck was taken up by a large green cabin with four windows. At the back end of the lower deck was a lifeboat.

The Littles took the lifeboat out. They needed room for something else — a walkie-talkie radio. The radio, five inches high with a one-foot antenna, fit neatly into the space.

The radio was one of a pair that belonged to Henry Bigg. The Littles had borrowed it. The other radio was in the attic of the Biggs's house. The radios were an important part of the expedition.

The plan was for Cousin Dinky and Della to keep an eye on the expedition from the glider. If they saw anything strange or dangerous, they would fly back to the house and radio to the boat from there.

While the others were getting the boat ready, Mrs. Little and Granny Little were busy too. They were packing sleeping bags, clothing, and food.

The food had to be sneaked out from the Biggs's kitchen. Dry foods were best: cornflakes, raisins, powdered milk, dates, sugar, dried beef.

Everything was packed into watertight containers — little plastic cans that rolls of film had come in. Mr. Bigg used a lot of film to take pictures and he always threw the containers away. The Littles had taken them out of the trash and saved them.

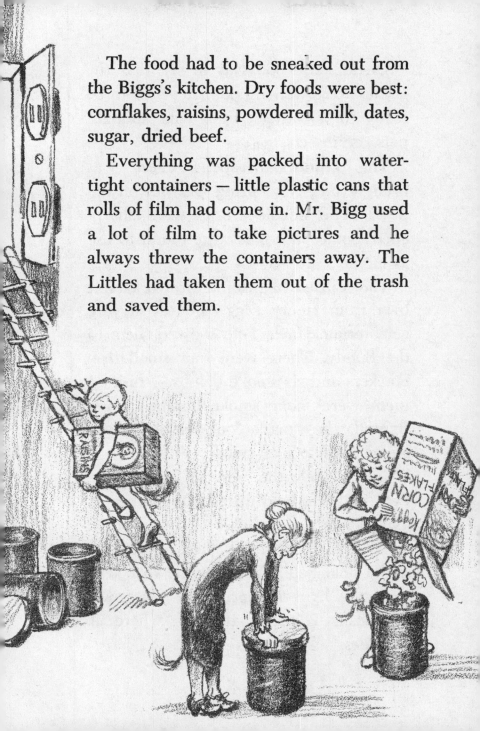

Uncle Pete's job was to see that the Littles were well-armed. They had to be ready for an attack from wild animals, pets, or insects.

The family's weapons chest was brought out. New string was put on the bows. The needle-swords were sharpened. Some push-pins were found to use as daggers.

The Littles had some fireworks left over from Henry Bigg's Fourth of July celebration. Uncle Pete showed them to the family. There were four small firecrackers and six smoke bombs — three of them were *snake* smoke bombs. When lighted, they made long black snakes, along with lots of smoke.

"And here's the best of all!" Uncle Pete said. He held up a bottle-rocket. It looked like a firecracker tied to a stick.

"We have three of these beauties," said Uncle Pete. "You put the rocket in a bottle, light it, and away she goes. Whooosh! High in the air where it explodes."

"We can use it as a signal," said Tom.

Then Uncle Nick said: "I'm going to make Grandpa's submarine raft by following his directions."

"What for?" asked Uncle Pete.

"I have an idea," said Uncle Nick, "that if two of us float down the brook ahead of the boat, we might see what happened to Grandpa."

"Ah," said Uncle Pete. "You think the submarine raft might go the same way?"

"Right!" said Uncle Nick.

He set to work searching the attic for Henry Bigg's old set of wooden blocks. He needed two curved blocks for the raft. After that, he got a glass bottle with a metal screw-on top and some rubber bands.

The Littles rolled the bottle over to the edge of the brook. Then Uncle Nick put the submarine raft together: First, he placed the two curved blocks against the neck of the bottle and put the rubber bands around them. This made the floating part of the strange boat.

Then Uncle Nick made a ladder from two short pencils and put it inside the bottle. They would need this ladder to climb in and out.

To keep the bottle from tipping over in the water, Uncle Nick put two small stones inside. Finally he put the lid on the bottle. The lid would be used as a trapdoor, and would keep water from splashing into the submarine.

When it was all finished, the submarine raft was put into the brook near the plastic boat. The bottle part went

under the water. The wooden part floated on top like a raft.

"*I'm* riding in that submarine raft," said Tom.

"Tom!" said Mrs. Little. "Remember how you got seasick on the sailboat?"

"Let the boy try it," said Uncle Nick. "After all, he was trapped in that sailboat and treated roughly. That's why he got seasick. He won't have any trouble at all on the raft."

"Do you really think so?" Tom asked.

"I'm sure of it," Uncle Nick said.

It was early morning. The Littles were all set to begin the exploring trip to find out what happened to Grandpa Little.

The sun had just come up. It was burning off the fog that formed during the night near the brook.

Granny Little stood on deck at the front of the boat. (She wanted to be sure and see everything.) "I'm glad I named the boat *Discoverer*," she said.

"A good name," said Uncle Pete. He stood with Lucy near the anchor string. He was wearing a sailor's cap and a life jacket made from a cork that had been hollowed out. (All the Littles wore these life jackets; it was one of Grandpa Little's ideas.)

Mrs. Little was in the cabin fussing over Baby Betsy. "She didn't get enough sleep," said Mrs. Little. "She'll be cranky all day."

Mr. Little sat in the captain's chair at the wheel. He looked at the sky. "I hope Dinky gets here soon," he said. "We should be on our way."

In the water nearby was the submarine raft. The Littles had tied leaves and twigs to the raft. They hoped that any big person or animal who saw it would think it was a piece of driftwood.

Tom and Uncle Nick were to travel on ahead of the boat in the submarine raft. If they saw any danger in the water, they would signal to the boat. That might give the other Littles enough time to hide the boat along the shore.

Suddenly a shout went up from the submarine raft: "There they are!"

Everyone looked up.

Cousin Dinky and Della zoomed overhead in their blue and white glider. Della waved from the back seat. The glider circled the boat once and flew off down the brook.

Everyone on the boat ran to the side and looked over the railing. The submarine raft was already headed down the brook. Uncle Nick worked with a long pole trying to keep going straight. Tom helped steer with a paddle made from a wooden ice cream spoon.

"Let's go!" cried Mr. Little. "We don't want them to get too far ahead."

Uncle Pete and Lucy pulled in the anchor. The *Discoverer* began to drift down the brook.

Uncle Pete called to Mr. Little: "Steady as you go, Will — there's a big rock on your starboard side."

Mr. Little laughed. "I see it. You mean it's on our *right* side, don't you?" he asked.

"Aye, aye sir!" said Uncle Pete.

"Okay," Mr. Little said. The tiny man turned the wheel hard to the left. The boat swung slowly over that way. They missed the rock.

"Gee!" said Lucy. "It's a good boat, isn't it?"

"Low bridge ahead!" Mr. Little called.

Sure enough, the *Discoverer* was moving quickly toward a low footbridge.

"There's plenty of room," said Uncle Pete. "That bridge is two feet above the water."

Lucy looked up. "What about the radio antenna?" she asked.

"Oh!" said Uncle Pete. He yelled: "Will! — the antenna!"

Mr. Little dropped the wheel. He ran to pull down the antenna. And just in time too, as the boat went under the bridge.

"Rubber tire stuck in the brook ahead!" sang out Uncle Pete.

Mr. Little ran back to the wheel. He turned it hard to the left. "This isn't easy," he said. "We'd better keep our eyes open."

"You try and keep your eyes on what lies ahead, Will," Uncle Pete said. "I'll take care of everything else."

"I've lost sight of the submarine raft," Mr. Little said. "It's gone around the bend up ahead."

"Here come Cousin Dinky and Della!" Lucy yelled.

The tiny glider came sailing along. As it passed over the boat, a small package fell. A parachute opened above the package.

Uncle Pete grabbed a pole with a fishhook on the end. He hooked the parachute out of the air as it drifted down alongside the boat.

"Perfect!" said Mr. Little. "Our first message."

Uncle Pete opened the package. Lucy and Granny Little came over to hear the message.

"STOP IMMEDIATELY!" read Uncle Pete. "CHILDREN PLAYING NEAR BROOK AHEAD."

By this time the boat was almost to the bend in the brook. Mr. Little steered it into the shallow water along the side of the brook. The tall grasses there made a good hiding place.

Uncle Pete pushed the anchor over the side.

They could hear children's voices nearby.

Mr. Little climbed from the boat. "Come on," he said. "Let's see what's going on. Nick and Tom are around that bend somewhere."

Uncle Pete and Lucy followed Mr. Little. They ran along the shore to the bend in the brook. Mr. Little crouched down behind a beer can. He held his finger to his lips. "Sh!"

There, a few feet ahead, some children were throwing rocks into the water.

"Let's break it to pieces!" shouted one boy. He threw a large stone; the water splashed — a piece of driftwood spun around in the water.

"I'll get it this time!" yelled another boy. He raised an arm to throw. "Watch this!"

"Oh my goodness!" said Mr. Little.

"It's the submarine raft!" Uncle Pete said. "Those nasty brats are trying to hit it with rocks."

"Oh, poor Tom!" said Lucy.

"Back to the boat!" said Mr. Little. "We've got to rescue Tom and Nick!" He grabbed Lucy's hand and ran. Uncle Pete limped after them as fast as he could.

They climbed aboard the *Discoverer.*

"Get out the weapons chest, Uncle Pete!" said Mr. Little. "Lucy — you and your mother and Granny lift up the anchor. We've got to get going."

In a few moments the boat was moving forward. Uncle Pete opened the weapons chest. "What now?" he asked.

"Send up one of those firecracker rockets," said Mr. Little. "Aim it so that it will go over the children's heads and behind them. Let's hope they run back to see what it is. Then we can slip through to find Nick and Tom."

Uncle Pete got one of the rockets and a match. "Lucy — you'll have to hold the bottle just as I tell you," he said.

"Hurry!" said Mr. Little. "We're coming to the bend in the brook. They'll see us."

The bottle was too heavy for Lucy. Granny Little and Mrs. Little helped her hold it in the right way.

Uncle Pete lit the rocket and dropped it in the bottle.

WHOOOOSH! The rocket flew high up into the sky. It arched over the children's heads, leaving a trail of smoke.

The big children didn't see the rocket. It fell toward the ground behind them.

BANG!

"Hey!"

"What was that?"

"A firecracker!"

"Someone's shooting firecrackers."

"Let's see who it is."

The children dropped their rocks and ran away from the brook.

The *Discoverer* came around the bend. It floated toward the place where the children had been. But the sub-marine raft was nowhere to be seen.

"Hello — this is Glider calling *Discoverer*."

"It's Cousin Dinky and Della," Lucy said, "on the walkie-talkie."

Uncle Pete limped over to the radio. He pushed the "talk" button. "Hello, Dinky — this is Peter."

"We'd better use code names," Cousin Dinky's voice came back, "in case someone's listening."

"Okay, Glider," said Uncle Pete. "Roger."

"What happened?" asked Cousin Dinky. "Is everyone all right?"

"We can't find the submarine raft anywhere," said Uncle Pete. "We've looked and looked, but they've disappeared."

"What are you going to do now?" asked Cousin Dinky.

"We're going on," said Uncle Pete. "We figure they must be ahead of us *somewhere*."

"Maybe you'd better stop so we can fly there for a look-around," Cousin Dinky said.

Mr. Little spoke into the radio: "No — we're coming to the Dark Woods. You stay where you are. You wouldn't be able to see much from above the trees. If we run into any trouble we'll give you a call on the walkie-talkie."

"All right — we understand," said Cousin Dinky.

"Good luck, everyone!" It was Della on the walkie-talkie.

"Roger, Della . . . er . . . sorry — *Glider*," said Uncle Pete.

A shadow fell over the boat.

"This is it," said Mr. Little. "The Dark Woods."

"Oh dear," said Mrs. Little.

"I wish we could find Tom," said Lucy.

Suddenly: "What's that?"

It was Granny Little. She stood at the front of the boat pointing to the water.

"It's Tom!" yelled Lucy.

"He's swimming!" said Uncle Pete.

Mr. Little turned the *Discoverer* toward the tiny swimming figure.

"There's *something* after him!" screamed Lucy. "What is it?"

"Looks like a turtle," said Uncle Pete. "Probably a snapping turtle."

"Oh, what are we going to do?" said Mrs. Little.

The boat raced toward the boy and the turtle.

Uncle Pete grabbed up a bow from the weapons chest. He fitted an arrow to the bowstring. He drew back an arrow, aiming at the turtle.

Zing! went the arrow.

It sailed over the turtle's head and landed in the water.

"Hurry, Daddy — hurry!" pleaded Lucy. "Save him."

"Someone *do* something," said Mrs. Little.

Granny Little ran to the weapons chest and grabbed for the first thing she could find. She pulled out a spear. The old lady threw the spear over the railing at the turtle. It flopped into the water. However, the turtle saw the splash and stopped for a second.

In that moment Mr. Little drove the *Discoverer* between the boy and the turtle.

At the same time, Uncle Pete hit the turtle on its shell with a long pole. The turtle dived underwater and swam off.

Lucy leaned over the railing. "Tom! Tom!" she cried. "Get out of the water. Hurry!" And then: "Mother! Daddy! *It's not Tom!*"

The Littles watched as the tiny boy — whoever he was — swam off for the shore.

"Well, I'll be —" said Uncle Pete. He took off his sailor's cap and scratched his head. "Look at that boy go! He swims like a fish. Who on earth is he?"

"Oh dear," Mrs. Little said. "I was sure it was Tom." She began to cry. "Are you *sure* it wasn't Tom?"

Granny Little put her arm around Mrs. Little. "There, there," she said. "We'll find them. Wherever they are, Nick and Tom can take care of themselves."

Tom and Uncle Nick were hiding in some bushes near the shore, behind an old cookie tin. They had been forced to jump off the submarine raft when the boys started throwing rocks at them. Luckily they were wearing their cork life jackets and had been able to swim to shore without being seen.

After the firecracker went off and the children left, Uncle Nick and Tom made their way through the bushes and back to the brook.

The submarine raft was gone.

"It must have sunk," said Uncle Nick. "Let's get back and find the *Discoverer*."

"Uncle Nick!" yelled Tom. He pointed. *"There it is! They've gone by!"*

Uncle Nick turned to look. He was just in time to see the green and white boat disappear around the next bend in the brook.

"Hold it!" Uncle Nick called out. He held out his hand as if to stop the boat.

"That's not fair," said Tom. "Wait for us." He began to run.

"Stop, Tom!" said Uncle Nick. "You'll never catch up. They probably think we're somewhere on ahead. Now what do we do?" He stopped to think.

Suddenly Uncle Nick snapped his fingers. "I've got it! Come on, Tom — back to the bushes."

Uncle Nick led Tom back to where they had just been hiding. He pointed to the cookie tin. "We're going to ride in this."

"Gee," said Tom. "That's a neat idea."

"Give me a hand, Tom," said Uncle Nick. "We've got to drag this thing into the water."

The two tiny people pushed and pulled and tugged at the cookie tin. Finally they got it into the brook.

Uncle Nick cut himself another long pole from a twig. Tom found his paddle nearby. They climbed into the cookie tin and pushed off from shore.

Tom paddled. Uncle Nick pushed with the long pole. They kept the cookie-tin boat going. It wasn't easy. The cookie tin bumped into rocks and spun around as it bobbed along.

Uncle Nick kept an eye out for Cousin Dinky's glider. "If Dinky comes along," he said, "he can fly ahead and stop the others."

After a while they entered the Dark Woods.

The water was deep and calm under the giant hemlock trees that were all along the brook. The branches of the trees kept out most of the sunlight.

In some places the sun broke through and turned the deep green of the water a warm yellow-green. Everywhere there were lichen-covered rocks, stony ledges, and smooth water-worn pebbles.

Green moss and ferns grew along the sides of the brook. One side was flat and one was hilly. The mosses and ferns covered the ground, the rock ledges, and the stumps of old trees like a soft blanket.

Uncle Nick whistled. "This is a most beautiful place," he said.

"Uncle Nick," whispered Tom. "I have a funny feeling."

Uncle Nick had stopped poling when they got to deep water. "What do you mean, Tom?" he asked.

"I feel that someone is watching us," whispered Tom. Suddenly: "There! On shore — did you see those shadows move?"

Two quick splashes behind them.

Tom and Uncle Nick turned to look. There were waves on the quiet water of the brook.

"Animals, maybe," Uncle Nick said.

"I wish we had some weapons," said Tom.

The cookie-tin boat floated on. Now they were deeper into the Dark Woods.

Suddenly Tom grabbed his uncle's arm. "There it is!" he said.

It was the *Discoverer*. The green and white boat was anchored near the hilly side of the brook.

"I don't see anybody," said Tom.

Tom and Uncle Nick paddled carefully over to the boat. The tiny pair jumped from the tin raft onto the boat.

After a quick look around, Uncle Nick said: "Everything is okay. They must have gone to explore the place."

Tom bent over the weapons chest. "Plenty of weapons here," he said. "Why would they leave the boat without weapons?"

"Tom — I don't know," answered Uncle Nick. "I pray that everything is all right."

Uncle Nick picked up a bow. He put it over his shoulder. Then he picked up a container of arrows and tied it to his belt. "We'll find their trail," he said. "They can't be far."

Tom took a spear. "Let's go!" he said. In a few moments the two were on the land. Tom found footprints in some wet sand. The tiny footprints led to the roots of a tree on the bank of the brook.

"They went in there — in among those roots," Tom said.

Uncle Nick looked closely at the footprints. "I see *more* footprints here," he said. "Could there be others like us in this wild place? Are they friends or enemies?"

Tom looked scared. "I told you someone was watching us!" he said.

"Let's go," said Uncle Nick. "Our family may be in trouble." He started off. Tom was at his heels.

The two tiny people found a trail among the roots. It led up from the shore to the top of the bank. Here the ground was covered with ferns and mosses. The trail went on up the side of the hill.

Tom and Uncle Nick moved forward quickly. Up ahead — under a high rock ledge — they saw a crowd of tiny people dressed in green. Among the strangers were the missing Littles!

Uncle Nick got down on one knee. Tom crouched beside him. Slowly Uncle Nick took the bow from his shoulder. He fitted an arrow to the bowstring.

At that moment, some of the tiny

people saw them. They pointed and yelled.

Suddenly Mr. Little broke away from the crowd. He ran toward Tom and Uncle Nick. "Tom! Nick!" he shouted. "Am I glad to see you!"

Uncle Nick stood up.

"We're among friends," called Mr. Little. "Put your weapons away."

Uncle Nick put his bow down. He and Tom started forward. "Thank goodness," said Uncle Nick. "Friends."

"Yes," said Mr. Little. He was smiling. "Come and meet the Brook Tinies — a most remarkable people. And what's more — we have great news! Grandpa Little has been here before us."

Tom and Uncle Nick were back with their family. Everyone talked at once:

"What happened? Where were you?"

"Yes, but where were *you*?"

"...and the rocket went up, WOOOOSSHH!"

"We heard the big bang!"

"...then Granny threw a spear."

"Granny threw a *spear*?"

"A cookie-tin ?"

"Grandpa was here?"

"He went on down the brook. He never returned."

After the noisy meeting, Mr. Little introduced Uncle Nick and Tom to some of the Brook Tinies. ". . . and this is Mr. Eddy Burns," said Mr. Little. "We met him after running into his son — a wonderful swimmer with a pet turtle. Mr. Burns is the proud father of twenty children."

"Twenty!" said Tom. "Wow!" He looked at Lucy. "I guess these kids are never lonely."

Mr. Burns was a tall, thin man. "And please call me Long Eddy, Mr. Little," he said. "All my friends do."

"The Burns family has invited us to lunch," said Mr. Little.

A group of the youngest Burns children stood near their father. They nodded their heads.

Uncle Nick looked around. "Where do you live, Mr. Burns?" he asked. "I don't see any . . ."

"We were just showing your family where we live when you came along,"

Mr. Burns said. He pointed to the nearby rocks and cliffs. "These rocks are full of caves. We live in them."

"Caves!" said Tom. "Wow!"

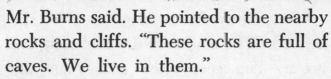

"They are limestone caves," Mr. Burns went on. "They were made by water draining down the hill for millions of years. It amazes me to think about it: Our homes were being prepared for us all that time before we got here. We're very thankful."

"But aren't they damp?" asked Uncle Pete. "All that water going through. My goodness!"

Long Eddy Burns laughed. "No, sir," he said. "The caves are dry and snug and warm. You see, years and years ago when our forefathers came here, they changed the way the water flows. It now goes *around* the rocks and misses the caves. Except for some that we let go through for cooking and washing."

"Where is Mrs. Burns?" asked Mrs. Little.

"You'll meet her at lunch," said Mr. Burns. "As soon as we saw your boat we sent word to her that we would have company for lunch."

Mr. Burns began walking. "Come and meet the rest of the family."

Mr. Burns led the way. He walked toward one of the many caves in the rock ledges.

Just then something fell from above. It splashed in the brook below.

Uncle Pete ducked. "What was that — a rock?" he asked.

Long Eddy Burns laughed. "That was one of the children diving," he said.

Uncle Pete limped over to the edge of the rock ledge. He looked down. "Why, we are at least six feet above the brook," he said. Then he looked up at the overhead ledge. "And did he dive from higher up?"

"He certainly did," Mr. Burns said. "Everyone can dive from where we're standing."

Mr. Burns pointed to a branch of a tree high above the brook. "Now, if you'd like to see a *really* high dive, keep your eyes on our neighbor, Sally Sikes — she's in that tree."

The Littles looked up at the tree.

"I don't see her," said Lucy.

"There — I see her. On that flat branch," said Tom. "Way up there."

"I don't believe it!" said Granny Little.

"I'm not looking," said Mrs. Little. She closed her eyes. Baby Betsy — in her mother's arms — reached up and touched her face.

"That's a ten-foot dive," Uncle Nick guessed.

The tiny diver leaped from the tree. The Littles clapped when the girl hit the water. It was a clean, beautiful dive.

"It must take years of practice to be able to do that," said Mr. Little.

"All Brook Tinies begin swimming before they learn to walk," said Mr. Burns. "We love the water. We live in the water a lot. And we get much of our food from the water, as you will learn at lunch." The tiny man entered the cave. He was followed by his children and the Littles.

If the Littles were expecting to see a dark and gloomy cave home, they were surprised. Instead they found the Burns's home to be a warm, friendly-looking place.

First, there was plenty of light. Beeswax candles were burning everywhere. The candlelight reflected off smooth cave walls. The walls were bright with many different colored rocks.

In the largest room of the cave the Littles met Mrs. Burns and the rest of the family. There were aunts, uncles, cousins, and grandparents. There were even some great, great grandparents. (Brook Tinies lived to be very old.)

Everyone sat at two long tables. Tom and Lucy sat with the Burns children. They told each other stories of tiny life.

The food was delicious. Everything was wild and came from the brook or nearby. First they had elderberry waffles and honey. There was wild rice, a watercress salad, and the tender sweet roots of the yellow goatsbeard plant.

They were served dishes of crayfish, mussels, and fish (tiny troutlings). Everything came in dishes and pots made of the clay found on the banks of the brook.

Voices carried well in the rock cave. People spoke softly. Even the hard-of-hearing had no trouble hearing what was said from one long table to the other.

After eating, Mr. Burns rapped on the table for attention. He stood up and talked for a long time. He said how wonderful it was to visit with Grandpa Little's relatives.

He thought Grandpa was a fine man. He hoped he was safe somewhere.

After that Mrs. Burns rapped on her table. She too stood up and talked for a long time. Mostly she told about the danger of going down the brook. She tried to talk the Littles out of making the trip.

Mr. Little saw that it was the thing to make speeches at Brook Tiny meals. So, he rapped on the table and stood up.

"Good! Let's hear from Will Little," said Long Eddy Burns.

Mr. Little said: "I suppose you would all like to know what it's like to live with big people." He talked for a long time about the Biggs.

Then he said how much he liked the Brook Tiny way of life. He said: "Living in the beautiful Dark Woods and swimming all the time must be very good for all of you. You look great!"

Finally Mr. Little said they would go ahead with their plan to explore the brook. "After lunch we will start out again," he said. "We've come this far safely. We have a good boat, and we're going to finish what we've started. It's our duty to find out what happened to Grandpa Little, and we're going to do it."

Everyone stood up and applauded.

Next, Uncle Pete stood up and made a speech. He talked about his favorite subject: the Mouse Invasion of '35. He went on and on, going over every part of the story. Finally, when some of the older Brook Tinies fell asleep and the children began sneaking out of the room, Mr. Little stopped him.

"It's time to finish, Uncle Pete," he said. "We really have to be leaving."

To finish up, Uncle Pete made a toast. Everyone raised a mug of apple cider.

"Here's to the friendship of all the Tinies in the Big Valley," he said. "To House Tinies, Tree Tinies, Wood Tinies, Trash Tinies, and especially to Brook Tinies."

Everyone clapped and cheered. The echoes of the applause bounced off the cave walls. They almost deafened everyone: everyone except Granny Little, who was hard-of-hearing anyway.

She liked it. "I think my hearing must be getting better," she said. "Everything is so clear."

The Littles were back on the *Discoverer*. They had been exploring for ten minutes when it began to rain.

At first the Littles hardly noticed the rain. They were still in the shade of the Dark Woods, and an umbrella of trees kept the rain from them.

But, behind them, where there weren't as many trees, the water rose quickly. It flowed into the brook from all sides.

The rising water reached the *Discoverer*. Mr. Little was surprised by the force of it. He fought to steer the boat toward shore. It wouldn't go. Finally he yelled: "Everyone to the cabin. Hold on to something. The boat is out of control!"

The Littles huddled together in the cabin of the boat. They held on to each other and to anything that was fastened down. The boat bobbed like a cork in the swirling water.

By now the overhead trees were water-soaked. The rain was coming down so hard the Littles could hardly see. From somewhere up ahead, the Littles heard a loud howling horn.

Then — suddenly — everything went black: as black as a moonless night. The boat raced forward, still out of control. A new and terrifying noise was all around them: CLICKETY CLACK! CLICKETY CLACK!

Then — in a flash — it was light again.

Through the pouring rain Tom could see a large, black, rushing shape. Suddenly he knew what it was.

"For heaven's sake!" cried Mrs. Little. "What's happening?"

"It's a train!" yelled Tom.

"I saw it too, Tom," said his father.
"We've just passed under a train through
some kind of underground pipe."

"Oh!" cried Mrs. Little. "I thought it
was the end of us." She hugged Baby
Betsy.

The water was calmer now. Mr. Little
climbed to the top deck. He got into
the captain's chair behind the wheel.
He hoped he would be able to steer the
boat once again.

That was when Mr. Little noticed
they weren't in the brook any longer.
The *Discoverer* was right in the middle
of a wide, rough *river*.

"There's land in front of us!" yelled Lucy.

"It's an island," said Tom. "We're heading straight for it."

"Uncle Pete!" yelled Mr. Little. "Get Cousin Dinky on the radio."

"Uncle Pete is seasick," Tom said. "I'll do it." The tiny boy pushed the "talk" button on the walkie-talkie. "Cousin Dinky — we're going to crash! Cousin Dinky, are you there?"

"Tell him where we are, Tom," said Mr. Little. "He should know where we are if we have to be rescued."

"I can't get him, Dad," said Tom. "He doesn't answer." He turned back to the radio. "Cousin Dinky — we're going to crash on an island. It's in the middle of a river. The river is past the Dark Woods and beyond the railroad tracks . . . somewhere. Please listen. We're going to crash!"

Just then a great wave struck the boat and lifted it right out of the water.

The next thing the Littles knew, their flat-bottomed boat was on the beach of the island.

"Is everyone all right?" asked Mr. Little. He ran from person to person.

Everyone was still on board. Except for bumps and bruises and some seasickness, the Littles were safe and sound.

"Thank God!" said Mr. Little. He turned to Tom. "Now, Tom," he said. "Get back on that radio. We have to reach Cousin Dinky."

Uncle Nick was looking over the boat. "This old tub will never float again," he said. "She's cracked and there's water leaking in."

"Dad!" yelled Tom. "It's gone! The radio is gone!"

"Oh, no — it must have fallen overboard on that last wave," Mr. Little said. "We're in big trouble."

Mrs. Little began to cry.

"Maybe we'd be better off if we had all sunk in the river," said Uncle Pete.

"Fiddlesticks and nonsense!" said Granny Little. "Don't be a big crybaby. We're alive and no one is badly hurt. I say, where there's life there is always hope."

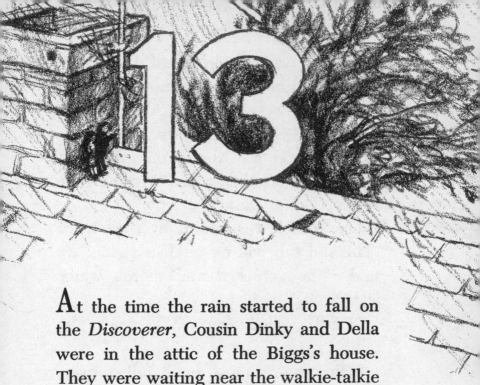

At the time the rain started to fall on the *Discoverer*, Cousin Dinky and Della were in the attic of the Biggs's house. They were waiting near the walkie-talkie in case the Littles should call in.

When he heard the rain, Cousin Dinky pushed open the trapdoor shingle to the roof. He and Della went out on the roof for a look around. They stood near the chimney trying to keep dry.

"Look at that sky!" Della said. "One minute the sun is shining, then suddenly it's raining cats and dogs."

"I think it's one of those quick, hard rains," said Cousin Dinky. "It won't last long. We'd better get back."

They ran for the secret door and climbed through into the attic.

Suddenly the lights came on. There were voices.

It was Henry Bigg and a friend coming up the attic stairs.

"We might as well play with the electric train," Henry said. "Darn the rain anyway!"

Cousin Dinky and Della hid behind a box near the walkie-talkie. They waited for the two boys to get what they wanted and leave the attic.

Then Henry's friend said: "Let's set it up right here. There's lots of space."

"Hey — that's a neat idea," Henry said. "We can use *all* the track up here in the attic. Wait'll you see this! We can spread it all over the place." He began pulling train boxes out into the center of the attic.

"Oh, oh," said Cousin Dinky. He whispered to Della: "This is bad news."

"How can we send a message with them around?" asked Della.

The two big boys began laying the electric train track on the attic floor.

"We'd better move the walkie-talkie," said Cousin Dinky. He got hold of the radio.

But it was too late; Henry was almost on top of them. Cousin Dinky and Della ran and hid.

Henry put the electric transformer near the walkie-talkie.

"He's right in our way," said Cousin Dinky. "He's almost *sitting* on the radio."

"If the *Discoverer* calls," said Della, "Henry Bigg will hear."

Now the train was on the track, chugging around the attic floor.

"If only we could get to the walkie-talkie!" Della said. "We could radio to the others and warn them not to call in right now."

"I have an idea," Cousin Dinky said. "If I pull the tracks apart, that will cut the electric current and stop the train.

While the boys are looking to see what's wrong, maybe you can send a message to the boat."

"But they will *see* you!" said Della.

"No, they won't," said Cousin Dinky. "See that tunnel on the other side of the attic? I'll sneak in there and do it."

It was a long way to the tunnel. Cousin Dinky ran from box to trunk to picture frame. Then he saw a way to go faster. Just at the right time — when he couldn't be seen — he dashed to the train and climbed aboard the caboose.

The train entered the tunnel and Cousin Dinky jumped off. He pulled at the tracks to get them apart. He couldn't do it!

He tried again; it took more strength than he had. Then he tried prying the tracks apart with a pencil. They still wouldn't budge.

The train was coming around again. Cousin Dinky had jammed the pencil down between the tracks and couldn't pull it out. He ran from the tunnel at the last moment.

The train entered the tunnel, hit the pencil, and flipped over. Box cars, oil

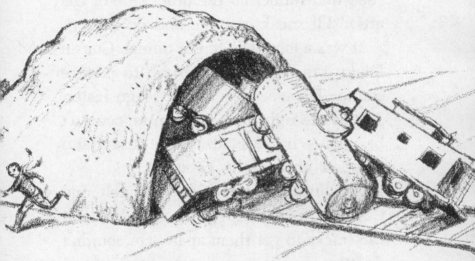

tankers, flat cars, and coal cars piled up on top of each other.

Henry Bigg ran across the attic floor. "I hope nothing's broken," he said.

"Wasn't that the coolest?" said the other boy. "Let's do it again."

"Are you joking?" shouted Henry. "I don't want my train broken, you dummy!"

Both boys yelled at once.

Della was hiding a few feet from the walkie-talkie. She started forward. Suddenly — while the boys were yelling — she heard Tom on the radio. What was he saying? Della ran. She got to the radio just in time to hear the last part of Tom's message:

". . . is past the Dark Woods and beyond the railroad tracks . . . somewhere. Please listen. We're going to crash!"

Della pushed the "talk" button. "Hello, Tom," she whispered. "Repeat the message. Where are you? What's happened?"

No answer.

Later, after Henry and his friend went away, Cousin Dinky and Della tried again.

There was no answer.

"Della — now think hard," said Cousin Dinky. "You've got to remember exactly what you heard Tom say. It may be our only chance to find them."

The rain had stopped. The Littles were together on the deck of the *Discoverer*. They were trying to decide what to do.

Suddenly they heard a yell:

"Hey there! You on the boat! Who are you?" It sounded like the voice of a tiny person!

The Littles looked toward the voice. There were three tiny people standing in the grass about five feet off.

"We're the Little family," Mr. Little called. "We're House Tinies . . . on an exploring trip."

One of the tiny strangers walked toward the boat. The Littles saw that he was an old man with a long, white beard.

He was dressed in animal skins.

"Will!" the old man shouted in a strong voice. "Will Little! Is it really you? I can't believe it. You've come to rescue us."

"It's Grandpa!" shouted Tom. He jumped up and down.

"It is!" said Mr. Little. He rubbed his eyes, wondering if he was seeing things that weren't there.

"Well, bless my soul!" said Uncle Pete. "It's the old man. We've found the old man."

"Is it *him*?" asked Granny Little. The shouting had confused her. She leaned over the railing staring down.

Mrs. Little put her arm around Granny Little. "Oh, Granny — it is," she said. "I'm so glad for you."

"I *knew* he was alive," whispered Granny Little. "I always knew it."

In the joy of the next few moments, the Littles forgot they were shipwrecked. When they got around to talking about it, they found that Grandpa Little's trip was much like theirs. He too had been swept under the railroad and into the river.

"My submarine raft was a failure,"

said Grandpa Little. "I never could steer it right." He grinned. "But I was too stubborn to stop exploring once I got started."

Grandpa's two friends were Brook Tinies. They had shipwrecked on the island too.

"They got here about six months after I did," said the old man. "I always thought I wanted to be alone, but after six months of talking to myself, I was happy to have company."

"Is there no way off this island?" asked Mr. Little.

Grandpa Little shook his head. "This part of the river is full of rapids. The waves are always high and there are lots of rocks," he said.

The three tiny people showed the Littles how they lived. They had built a comfortable home. It was made from things that had washed up on the island. Bottles, boards, beer cans — everything — went into building it.

The house was built over a hollow
tree stump. Grandpa Little had invented
many things to make it comfortable. For
one thing, they had piped in water to
the house by using hollow reeds. In the
winter they kept a low fire burning
inside the tree stump. This kept the
house warm and snug during the coldest
winter days.

Everyone was standing on the porch of the tree-stump house when Tom looked up and yelled: "It's a glider!"

"Cousin Dinky!" said Uncle Pete.

"Thank heavens he's found us," said Mrs. Little.

"Not yet, he hasn't," said Mr. Little.

The glider passed directly over the island heading down the river.

"Quick," said Mr. Little. "Let's get the smoke bombs out."

The Littles raced to the beach. Tom was first to the boat. He ripped the lid off one of the film containers. The smoke bombs were still dry.

Mr. Little got a match from another water-tight container. One by one he lighted the six smoke bombs. Clouds of dark smoke drifted up into the sky. Black snakes grew out of three of the bombs.

The blue and white glider suddenly wheeled around in the sky. It turned back toward the island.

Everyone cheered.

"We're going home," said Mr. Little.

"Good old Dinky — he's found us," said Uncle Pete. "I knew he would."

Granny Little and Grandpa Little stood arm in arm. They smiled at each other. "And we found what we were looking for," said Granny Little. "It's the end of a perfect adventure."

"Oh golly — it's over," said Lucy. She smiled up at her father. "Can't we do it again sometime? Can't we?"